Of Stars And Bare Skin

Dawn Serbert

Copyright © 2020 Dawn Serbert

ISBN:9798622758850

DEDICATION

I dedicate this book to all the wonderful prompt hosts from Twitter.

All the poems have a prompt in, which inspired me to write.

CONTENTS

A collection of poems which I have written

for prompts on Twitter,

Some dark, some of love, some of grief

All from the heart and mind of me..

Everything Beautiful Bleeds

~

Everything beautiful bleeds
No bones
Of memory leave

A drown of last dismay
The gilded
Leaf of gold to stay

Of echoes
To haunt silently

A slip of time must weep

The dreams
Of dust beyond the sun

To sleep
And fall today..

Dust And Bones

~

All we are
Is debris of dust and bones
In the end,
Dispersed on the roads both taken
And abandoned..

New To Old

~

Now
I exit breath alone
To shed the dark from flesh
To bone
To leave discomfort
Where it's cold
As time moves forward
New to old..

Dark Cousin Of Reality

~

Ricocheting
From obstacles to differences

My restless soul
Becomes dismembered

Discarded

Mirroring a dark cousin of reality

A hybrid caught between
Formidable beyond reason

No longer here to dream..

Broken Mirrors

~

Broken mirrors
Hide my wrong doings
Refracting tiny
Glimpses of the layers within

If i dare to glance and dream darker

Will venous
Red wings of twilight
Cut my feet

Like quicksand binding

And drag me to the underworld
In a scatter of burning
Debris..

Death Can Steal

~

The days
After tomorrow
They are
Stories not even death
Can steal..

Invisible At Dawn

~

Something
Stealing the air

Transfering silence to my mind
In gunfire
Needles of plagued flares

Flickering
Darkened light to time

Neither lifeless yet unborn
Neither real nor an illusion

Reaching
For awareness

Locked invisible at dawn..

Carrying Me

~

Be my lungs
Tonight
My sheltered crevice
My hybrid
Between land and sea

Keep me lit
In dusks hour of recollection

For the shadows
Are choking
The light

The chimes counting down
To be free

Carrying me
Beyond where creation
Whispers

The dawn to breathe..

Death Surrounds

~

Death
Surrounds us
It does not become us
It simply
Moves us forward
We are never
Long lost
From our beginnings..

Intimate Vibrations

~

It's the
Scratching
Of a whisper biting just below
My skin

Dusks intimate vibration
Snapping
Glass strings to begin

Overcast
Elastic clouds
Firing raven clawed
Dark sin

Eternal
Midnight stirring
That creates me
From within..

Without The Dust

~

To stare at the sunset
Or the Dawn

How the colours
Would not be so beautiful
Without
The dust
That adorns them

How the shadows we walk
Would be
The blackest of ink

How the patch of the rain
Would be barren

How the splendor
We see
Would fall

Would simply
Abandon..

Savour The Taste

~

Don't think about it
It plays
Too much on your mind

Wait out the hunger

Savour the taste
As it dances
Inside

Chaos is wreckage
Clawing delirium's lock

Tribute the demons
The angels mislead you
Impulsive and wild

Run with the beauty of you
Your soul has never
Forgot..

Killer In You

~

Muffle your steps
The creeks of the board
Will hear you..

Silence steers loneliness
Seeds of dissent
You can't see..

Follow the blindfold
The pipers
Not here to save you..

Tender the dodge of the bullet

The killer in you
Is not free..

Angel's Touch

~

Judgement before
I steal time
Murmurs before I unlatch dialogue..
Holy water burns me
Seductive..
Close your eyes now
Hush..
The devils not in me..
The bridle was broken
Long ago..
With the breath of an Angel's
Touch..

That Is Love

~

Even
If we're just memories
A stitch
In the lens
Of the midnight calm
Caught between
The axis of life and death
Then that's enough
That is love..

Untethered

~

I rake
Away the wreckage
With rapture
Watching the dance of fireflies
Like golden confetti
Spiraling
The magic of forevers
Into beautiful falls
Of halcyon
Clarity
No thought to human error
As i run
Along the shoreline
Exquisitely
Untethered..

Darkway

~

Transmuted
To another dimension
Yet still the cries
I hear them

Swings and roundabouts
Swaying
Plagues of sorrow

But to find them
Is to lose myself to the darkway
Of my blackest moments

But to leave them
I would
Cut my soul to a redemption

I can't falter..

The Darkest Bloom

~

The darkest bloom
Lays inside me
Mirroring the caligo that haunts my eye
Almost like i'm a wilt
Wavering
Adrift in this astringent wasteland
Yet a stowaway of time
Unbandaged
Structured corrupt
Beyond death
With only a taste of my soul
To die..

Empty Air

~

Empty air
Is all there is now

Copper irises

Imperfect

The shadow that once held me
Outlawed

A marionette of me

Unhallowed

The dust of crow cries
The bones of rain
Where i slip

No hands to reach me
No trace of me

To follow..

Then There's Him

~

But then there's him..

Spiralling
Me down below the sodden dirt

Where the dark moves
In indigo and iris dreams

Retuning my mind
Making me feel

Splintering the bricks of my flesh
Where the wild flowers bloom
Unseen

Piece by beautiful
Fractured
Seam..

Forever In This Day

~

It's hushed here
Unruffled..

The whispers have fallen
The shadows

Have quietly crept away..

I can hear the ocean kiss
When the sun sets..

I can hear
The wings of the night birds
Oscillate

I can feel
The wild of the roses..

Forever

In this
Day..

Fly Away

~

They become transparent
My wings

Just like the skeleton
Flower's petals when it rains

I watch their
Metamorphic grace bloom

Watch their ivory
Frost wilt
To tender wisps

Watch the cut of their feathers
Fray

Somewhere
Between heaven and earth

Then I gently

Fly away..

Devil's Smile

~

I feel attached
Yet unrelated

Inebriated
To the blackness

Yet in love with the candlelight
Romance of dancing..

A midnight
Rage of fire burns inside me
Yet i am as cold as the bottled dusk
With the sublime
Of the wild chasing me

To find
A devil's smile..

Bloodstained Hours

~

Insomnia drinks
Into me
Sideways in its smile
Yet somehow
I am submissive
To its pleats of derangement
Collapsing around me

Camouflaged
As sanity beautifully forlorn

Like a
Thirst unending
Naked in its defiance
To seek
The dark bloodstained hours

Of Dawn..

Unfed

~

I suffer
Madness beautifully..

I disrobe
It down raw to razor lust bliss..

I dream in the black
Of the ashes of red

And let it bleed

Dark and sensuously
Over me

Kissing me

Unfed....

Undisturbed Winds

~

I scatter myself
In disembodied reflections
Of freedom..
To drift eternal on the symphonic
Resonance
Of undisturbed winds..

Swallow Your Words

~

Don't
Swallow your words
They will
Choke out your soul..
And the scavengers preying
Will reap all the golden
Verses..
Those half penny dreams
Will fall to..
Those fibrous ropes inside you..
Then how will you breathe
My darling..

How will I find you..

Wasted Mind

~

Out of the
Attics of my wasted
Mind..

Benumbed and soundless

Silhouettes
Lick to taste
The vice of stained
Hands..

Of Stars And Bare Skin

~

Of stars and bare skin
I am born
A crest of a silken wave..
A howl
Of the raging wind..
A haunt
Of an echoes graze..
In colours of sunlit motes of dust
I walk..
An eclipse of the soul..
Dancing
With moon fire
In balletic ripples
Of love..

Shadows

~

Do you ever
Watch shadows fall apart..
How they
Look like dark stars
Forming,
How their wisps drift gracefully
Into a union,
Resembling a soul of raven seas
Migrating to coral coves,
Only to then
Wash upon the sands lonely kiss,
Before again
Taking flight on the breeze..

Devil's Death

~

It itches me,
I want to scrub it off,

But then..

I like the feel of it.
The disturbingly
Bewitched magnet of its contact,

It's almost intimate..
Almost addictive..

Twisting
Ravenously over my flesh,

Teasing..

Imploring me to keep it,

This fiery hope
Of a devils

Death..

Something Virtual

~

Am i made
Of something virtual
Or am i made
Of something dark?
Something Unadorned
Crawling
From the stars?

Is my touch
A burn of paper sand?
A pixel for the whim
Of man?..

Am i real at all
In here.?.
How am I to understand...

The Soul Of Time

~

If for just one kiss
You would give me the world
I would graciously
Decline..
But if for a rose
That pierce of its eloquent thorns..
I would give to you..
The soul
Of time..

Hourglass Keepsake

~

She left me an hourglass keepsake,
Tied it with ribbons
Starlings and doves,
And hid it beneath the ivy trellis..

I had no concept
Of the value behind this message.
Until i awoke
And found her fallen..

And heard
Her haunting song
Of love..

I Fold Inside

~

In this stillness
I fold inside..
Crumbling in my ghost dome
Unsteady..
Capricious to the murmurs
Sweeping over my auditory senses,
Punishing the pain
As I try,
To retract the glass
Heart shards..

Permafrost

~

Permafrost..
I love with no heart,

Untouchable

Outside the barricades of concealment

A slither of a dream
Unhinged..

Ricocheting sideways
In every
Reflection
That

Begins..

It's Me

~

This feeling of humanity
Is breaking..

I want to rip it out
Crush it under the pendulums
Outward scream
To leave

But yet..

It bleeds such beautiful music
Twists the aria
Of twilight
To unlatch my eyes

Like kirlian photography..
It's developing,

It's me...

I Have No Voice

~

I have no voice

No words

Just silence as i try to speak

No form to my existence

No barricade to keep

I am inverted

Achromatic in my still of sleep

I am unborn

A mirror self of me..

The Silence Of The Soul

~

To know

The silence of the soul

To know the truth of who you are

For better

For worse..

You have to dissipate

Relinquish everything you thought

You knew..

Release the scars of earthbound

Shatters..

And let go..

Unending

~

This silence

A steal of rapture running so deep

That it collapses the very folds of time

To perfume my soul

And hold it there

Unending..

Love

~

There's

No stronger vibration

In the universe

Than love

No veil that can hold its path to seek

No chthonic darkness

That can tether its limits

Love is the very tide of time itself

Turning the galaxies lighting the stars

Love is the essence of everything

We are...

Uneven

~

How odd

The universe works in layers

We find uneven

Prompting questions that confuse

Our minds

Closing temporary curtains

Yet energy

Can never die

It's faded flame lies out of time

Until the moment

We know how or why – nothing

Is ever certain...

A Dream That Was Never Mine

~

What is ether

What is real

What lies beyond the boundaries

Of my mind to feel

I find myself floating freely

Wondering if my consciousness

Is aligned to me

Or is it existing far away

Somewhere else

Where i pulse and thrive

Inside a dream that was never mine..

Wear Death

~

Unstitching

My lips

I discover my words

No longer form in speech

Like a missing exit

Of a twisted labyrinth

I slept in between dark fates

Entering this burnished wasteland

Where I wear death

In a dream to awake..

Breathtaking

~

Words

Have no substance

Without the

Instruments of our ears

Our voice

Written with so many

Meanings

How we improvise the sound

The verse

Is our own personal choice

And that's

What makes them all the more

Breathtaking..

Discomfort
~

It's a lot

Like stripping

A bandage off

You've

Kept the scars

The pain

Hidden in comforting

Discomfort

But there comes

A time you have to bleed

Raw your name

To feel

And begin again..

Regret

~

The

Walls of regret

Crumble

Only when temper

Subsides

Into

Hushed cries..

Footprints Of You

~

Footprints

Of you

As i run my fingers

Down

The pages of our past

Lingering

Still

In a rustic redolence

That splinters

My soul

To remember..

Indigo Darkness

~

There

Are places

In the human heart

Where

Indigo darkness

Clings with

Unremitting glee..

As Dust

~

When

Our blood runs

As dust

When our minds

Light decays

The graves of the dead

Will disorder in a rage

Fire wraiths

Will soar

The veil will fall

And all that we are

Will cease

In a throw of darkness..

Intimate Sonnets

~

Sounds

Of hope scratch

The glass

Of my mind tonight

Murmuring

Vague

Intimate sonnets

Suffocating me

With delicious kisses and dusky

Blade dreams

Of inspiration..

Humans

~

I hear

Noises when i walk

It's the humans

How they talk

It's so loud it hurts my soul

I have to keep my self control

Their words

They have no meaning

No sense

Within their reasons

Benighted in the path they choose

Bleeding innocence

Disregarding truth....

I Falter

~

I falter

In my step

Torn

Between two existences

One a point

Of time

Pulling me to leave

The other

A broken mind

Not allowing me to breathe

Yet neither

One is kind

Neither sets me free..

Just Ghosts

~

He

Whispers

The ghosts are just angels

Visitors

Steering you through

Midnight dreams

Of decay..

Forgotten

~

Ominous

Maelstroms

Pulsate like dysfunctional

Clockworks

Over haunted bodies

Of water

Where time has been

Forgotten..

The Unconscious Sleep

~

In the

Unconscious sleep

Death answers

Primordial calls of degraded distortion

You have pledged

Seeking

To claim his pay

It's a waltz of time

Slipping through your fingers

For how long

Can you stay awake

Before you need to dream..

Lost Girl

~

To the

Naked eye

Am i a ghost

A shadow unheard

A lost girl

A lonely wolf

For i have no heartbeat

No skin to bare

Detached

From mortal discord

In a dream-like land

Blinking

Back confusion

Aware..

Undertow To Death

~

This

Wake i rove

Within

A sleep is complex

A hybrid

Dream of fire dust breath

Where time

Moves forward through

A vortex

And the chimera

Is my undertow to death..

Until Dusk

~

Until dusk

I am

Nothing to descry

No flesh to feel

No life to breathe

No substance to disclose

My eyes

Lost in dust wisps of memory

My soul – sunken

Dispossessed

Inside a hollow lullaby

Of eternities

Departed..

Until dusk...

Flesh To Heart

~

Pendulum

Blade

Swinging a trail of death

Motif eyes

Swaying right to left

Its burning

Appetite hidden inside twisted

Steals of dark

Its lust

For blood

A rage of love

Ripping flesh to heart..

Undress Me

~

Undress me

I am nobody

But the soul of who

I am

Disrobe my flesh

My bones

My chords of times cold hand

Return me to the darkness

Of the starlight serenade

Where i'm nothing

Yet i'm

Everything of creation

Unafraid..

Do You Really Know Yourself?

~

Wipe

Away the makeup

Set aside the mask

Stand

Before the mirror

A question you must ask

Do you

Really know yourself?

Every part of truth?

Would you like to meet yourself?

The ruse

That hides in you..

Midnight Dreams

~

I think

I'm an anomaly

In one galaxy

Or maybe many

A kindred soul living amongst

Un-living things

Perhaps

A mirror or myself

Or yourself

Or maybe just an angular momentum

Of an electron spin

Riding viking clouds of nebula

Lost in

Midnight dreams..

Dark Disgrace

~

Strip

My soul down

Naked

Take it to an eclipsing space

Watch me form into beloved disorders

Cut from

The deepest depths

Of dark disgrace..

Night Ambling

~

Dusk

Is my dawn

My muse of night ambling

Taking me

To sweeping indigo blades

Where I breathe its aroma

Devour its verse of twilight creatures

Uncurbing my brake

Allowing

Bridges of enchantment

To call

Forth old souls

Of the midnight cabaret..

Dark Existence

~

Where

The shadows comfort us

In their embrace

Below the unbalance of the world

We love

In cords of dark existence

Captive only

To the tempo of each other's soul..

Am I Made Of Stars

~

I am torn apart

Scattered

On bitter winds of empathy

Lost inside

A cyclone of twisted emotion

Understanding nothing

And yet

Above me the midnight reflections

How they sing

How they dance

Lighting the sky with such colours..

Are they me?

Am I made of stars..

I Still Reach

~

I still reach

Recalling your touch

A thousand

Kisses of dawn

Surrounding

Me in reveries of love

Soft sighing

Ghosts of a distant time

Sailing

Around me

Falling..

I still reach...

Fury

~

Fury

How it lacquers the tunnels

Of your mind with dark dexterity

Burning

Your words beyond rational breath

Twisting your touch into razor edge ribbons

That break

Achromatic senses to the thirst

Of the kiss of blood

Leaving behind the cry of sanity

To fall..

Velvet Ripples

~

The wind..

How I feel its howl..

Velvet ripples

Brushing against me

Dancing

With passions of whispering depths..

Spiraling

Perfumed kisses of tiger rain

Timeless..

Perfect over my breath..

Hallucinating Mercury

~

Hallucinating

Mercury across the still

I arrange

Maddening moonlight whispers

Of the soul

Harmonising midnights

Hollow breathing

In a torrent

Of ephemeral kisses

Touching

Finding

Smouldering passions burning

Across time..

They're Wrong

~

They're wrong

You know

When they tell you

You've

Lost your mind

That you've gone too far

In a delve

Of unusual structure

Because too far is exactly

Where

You're meant to be

Unfocused in imperfect pulls

Of chaos

For they're the depths that

Set you free..

Secret Harmony

~

Once a million moons ago

Rare flowers

Bloomed in the night

Painting

Notes of secret harmony

To enhance

Man's inner being

Songs of angels

Blew

Toward the lonely light

Sending waves of illumination

Into the dark..

It's a nostalgia

I find myself lost in

Often..

Umber Dirt

~

Verdant hillsides

Tumbling

Over umber dirt darkness

Aurora rose fire skies

Blazing the stars

To align

Oceans of electric blue tides

Pulling the moon to shadow & light

Lava raging below

So silent

So beautiful

So deadly

All turning the world

In breaths

In time..

Devil's and Madness

~

Undress

Me with Vivaldi's four seasons

Caress the skeletal

Strings

Of my thorns

As you play my chassis

Feral

Steering the trail of devil's and madness

Never stopping

Until time unravels

The deep

Of the dark rhyme

Of my poem..

Familiar

~

I've

Never been here before

Yet how familiar it is

Like a distinct feeling

Running through me that it's mine

Has it

Pulled me through

Or have I pulled it through?

For the shadows that smudge

Seem to be merging

Reality and dream alike

Mirroring the unknown..

Limitless

~

Limitless

We howl rage not calm

Seeking

Twisted dark desires

Nefarious

Cocktails of deaths pleasure

To anesthetize our

Conscience..

Sour Harvest

~

Breathe deeply

The air may be thin

But taste it's flavour

The sour harvest

The acrid scent

Feel it's primal howl awakening

And wonder no more

Why this freakishly beautiful bouquet

Lures you

To dystopia's dark descent..

Synchronized Ballet

~

Weaving

In and out of synchronized ballet

Like a flock of ghost starlings

Russet shadows

Lacquer the wild blue in explosions

Of ink blood engravings

Dusting dawns last golden hour

As they dance a midnight

Hue..

Spellbound

~

I drift

Through the firmament

Whispering

Goodbye to my substance

Lost

In this spellbound

Midnight light

Yet somewhere

In time

I am still

A kiss in the wind..

Borrowed Words

~

I have

Borrowed words from you

Arranged them

On the overhang of my mantlepiece

Just there near the hearth

Where the sun

Catches the windows arch

So that

When the rain ebbs and the sky

Clears to blue

They will light up

And just for a moment

I'll be with you..

Maya Blue Feathers

~

It was their silhouettes i saw first

Vivid patterns of chiffon white flocking the sky

In synchronization

Then maya blue feathers reaching out to me

With doleful black eyes and a silent whisper

It's something i will never forget

Something that left my soul...fragile..

Reflection Distorted

~

My reflections distorted

If i touch the glass it ripples like a butterfly effect

Caught in an hour lens

If i look beyond i see cut edge shards

Of my mirror self looking back with hollow unfed eyes

Searching everything over nothing to symmetrically

Loop time..

Something In The Air

~

There's

Something in the air

Rustling

The creases of twilight

To twist times

Clock of elegance beyond

The fringes

Of burning embers

Speaking a vocabulary

Unrestrained

Caressing me darkly

Unafraid..

A Loop Of Time

~

I drift a loop of time

Banished..

A blushing ember

Of a rose to comfort the void..

But the shadows

They distract me..

For how they gleam

How they

Speak of kaleidoscopic wanderings..

A bridging of the gap

Once unbeknownst..

Now known

To me..

Cherries And Dusk
~

Crimson

Tides of cherries and dusk

So provocative

So majestic

Makes me wanna run

With raven wolf eyes

Between

Below and above

Kissing

The dreams of broken riddles

Getting drunk on the night

Making love

Uninhibited..

Falling so beautifully

Misunderstood..

Wordless Mind

~

There are whispers

Born of the wordless mind

Rising from the depths

Calling to infiltrate your heart

Waiting for the newborn colours

Of poetry and the soulless

Touch of time

To fall as one / to fold as light

To speak in darkness

To dream tonight..

Tides Of Love

~

Our creed

Should fall to one of benevolence

Unfeigned and undressed..

For how

As we turn with the tides of love

Unto the arms

Of death

Can we be anything more

Or anything

Less..

Something New

~

I feel

The circles of the past

Unravelling

Where once was blood

Now runs a river of ice

Where once

Was sound now plays

A hollow cello

Of a dark enchanted dream

That speaks of something new

That speaks

That i am dead

Yet written

Unborn

Just out of truth..

The Dawn of Burning Glass

~

Every snowflake falls differently..

A star of us

A memory of our path..

Written

In the light that calls the darkness

Falling ice

That's ever changing

Giving us

The chance to see

That we

Are found within the dawn

Of burning glass..

Burnished Splinters

~

Burnished splinters..

I cut them

From my flesh..

Thorned and bleeding..

Perplexed

By the tears of velvet embers

They weep..

Watching them slip

In a waltzing harmony of redressed

Clarity..

Drifting them softly

To sleep..

Copper Bruises

~

I softly spiraled

Just

Like a spider branch

Dripping from the waters biting grave

Of copper bruises

Transmuting to mechanical indifference

Becoming the flesh

The bones

The blood

Of a paper doll

Contoured to a lullaby that echoed

The madness of a tethered

Soul..

Mandolins Song

~

Reflections of light

Dance like nets cast out to sea

Inside our eyes

Vibrating a mandolins song

Soft and low

A hidden tune just out of time

But no less real

Than winter's melting snow – it's

The one thing that makes us human..

Guardian Of The Woods

~

I find

Myself unrestrained

In closed

Secrets

A guardian of the woods

Lost in solitudes charm of tranquility

Where fairytale

Chimes

Scatter tales of coloured rain

Why would i want to return to a world

That's earthbound

When i'm reaching beyond reality

Unashamed..

Forget The Stars

~

He shows

Her the detour to heavens door

Whispering

" Forget the stars

they are made to shatter

This is my heart "

Forget To Feel

~

We live

Within an illusion

A state of error

Not knowing who or what is real

Not knowing

How to cope

Cornered in wheels

Of automated programmes

Running us to empty

Whilst boundaries

Rise in chaos around us

And in the midst of it all

We forget to feel..

Fear Your Sleep

~

Fear

Your sleep

For sleep shifts

To dreams

And dreams are lost hours

Where

Death is set free

But deaths not an ending

It's sanity's dormant cry

Threading

Your subconscious

To open your eyes..

Silent Slayers

~

They

Became a dependency

Silent slayers

Attacking me with with glassy dreams of rapture

I remember how they felt

Each one different

Spiraling

Invigorating

Yet destined to depart

Destined to expel

Until the last one took me further

Than the very place i fell..

No Voices

~

We liken

Our thoughts to think

We're empathic

But our behaviour suggests

We're estranged from that sentiment

For we'll

Smile at strangers

Give our hearts thoughtlessly

To digital corruption

Yet turn

A blind eye to the ones with no voices

And not even feel regret..

ABOUT THE AUTHOR

I has been writing poetry all my life

It's my passion

You can find more of my poems on Twitter @atreya2112

Printed in Great Britain
by Amazon

65981060R00061